"Move," Oscar says into Javi's ear. "Keep your hands up."

Hearing Oscar's voice like that, low and at his side, Javi can't help but lean over, choke his eyes shut and strain to keep the water in. Oscar has a smooth tone, syrup in the ear, and it makes Javi think of Marcel.

"Move. Don't block too much with your hands, they get tired. Twist at the hips and dip your shoulders. Don't shuffle your feet. Hands! Keep your fucking face covered," Oscar says.

Like Lou Rawls whispering in your corner, telling you how to shake the other man. Like the voice a person wants inside of him telling him what to do and how to do it. A tongue covered in honey. Marcel's tongue was thick and Javi can feel it now against the inside of his cheek mixed with the blood from the hook he took in the last round. Javi spits into a bucket and Marcel's tongue is gone.

"You hear me? Don't shut your eyes, we're not done yet. He hit you and now he thinks he knows how to beat you. Don't let him near your face. Keep your eyes open. Move your head. Watch and move. Cover up."

The bell rings and Javi gets up. He hops from his left foot to his right, bounces just a bit, the way he might have before climbing into bed with beautiful Marcel, already naked and waiting for him. Keep the hands up. Don't let him catch you. Don't let him get your pretty face.

*   *   *

Oscar knows this is just a practice bout and that he should let Javi be. The boy's got his real first fight in a few days. And he's got his other fighters to check up on, other men working the bag and jumping rope, waiting for Oscar to come by. The boy's got headgear, a fair partner, and a decent pair of gloves. But he's a sprinter, it seems. He likes getting after people and then running—no patience. Oscar knows what happens to these fighters. He makes them wear heavier gloves; makes them lift weights before they spar, makes them run a little extra to drag their legs down. No power and no bounce means no rioting in the ring. Too tired then, and all that's left are slow, steady jabs and well-placed hooks, body shots. The work of boxers, not anxious gunners.

And he knows Javi is anxious. His brother has been gone for what, just over a week? Buried two days ago on Sunday, the weather shitty because it's January, the ground frozen and cold. There was a fog working its way through the cemetery, and he and Javi stood together with all of Marcel's vendors. They watched the casket lower, slick with the moisture in the air. How many vendors did he have? Twenty-five? Thirty? Maybe more. Enough little Cuban coffee stands that he could do what he wanted during the day. Enough that he could drive around lazily and pick up boys the same time as checking in on business. Marcel the fucking entrepreneur.

"Oscar, I am the jéfe!" Marcel would shout. "My boys are on every corner. That bodega shit people are sick of. People know. You want a shot of café that'll get you hard, send you home to your lovely, then find one of my carts."

Oscar used to call his brother Ali, used to tell him his mouth was bigger than his face, and that the King of the World would have a hard time getting a word in when he was around. And somehow, though he'd never put on a pair gloves in his life, Marcel would quote the King, or something close to it.

"Cockadoodle, Oscar! I'm a crow that's seen the light. I have seen the light and I'm crowing! Fuck Paris— New York is the City of Lights!"

Oscar had to smile; never bothered telling Marcel it's the rooster that crows at first light. He was loud, though, so it made sense that Marcel was the caw rather than the bird itself. Marcel the rooster's crow, the goddamn king crow. And that was even before Oscar moved up north with him. Marcel used to squawk over the phone when Oscar was still in Miami with their mother, Agueda. He'd scream across the line about how bright the lights were, how the city never ended, and, more often, how much he loved the boys.

"Oscarito! You've got no idea, man, what it's like here. You have to come see this place. The beaches are too hot in Miami, and everybody's got a tan. But the bodies here—you can have a different body every night!"

"Is that all you do up there, Muchi? Chase little boys?" Oscar asked.

"Hermano, you sound like Mamá. I got ten coffee stands now, and the borough loves me. The city loves my espresso cubano. Don't joke—como está, Mamá?"

"I think she misses you, but she don't say much about it."

It didn't seem such a lie. Agueda was a small, round woman, and she got smaller when Marcel left; her shoulders fell forward, the same reaction she'd had to their father's heart attack when the boys were ten and twelve. Oscar remembers the day after Papi's funeral, the day she crowned Marcel king. He remembers perfectly the cousins crammed into their quaint Hialeah living room chewing stewed tomatoes and watching as Agueda went to kiss Marcel on the forehead. It wasn't one of those sad, infantilizing, mother-hen pecks, either. It was a coronation kiss, quick and deferential, and Oscar knows Marcel didn't see it coming, a hooking lip, a sign to everyone watching with mojo agrio dripping from the corners of their fat mouths, Marcel included, that Agueda still had her sons, had the son who would now be the man of the house. They'd be just fine; they'd slide right down the pecking order and Marcel, the youthful, fair-skinned image of their father, would, from then on after, sit next to Mamá Sundays at San Miguel and hold her hand during the Lord's Prayer. For years he did. But when Agueda speaks of Marcel now, it's not so pleasant: "My son the marica, don't know the difference between díos and diáblo." Her beautiful boy, her cariño, the one who'd come home from high school one afternoon with a busted face because he'd been caught with his hands in another boy's pants. Marcel told her then, and she damn near went.

"Maybe you should take a break from the boys and try coming home," Oscar said.

"Soon, maybe." Always the same empty promise, as if Hialeah had never been, as if Marcel had sprouted from the stone pillars of New York, some magical love-child so rooted in skyscrapers and subways that the city would die without him. As if the lights would all go out if he ever crossed the river and headed south again.

But then, "Or you, Oscarito, could come up here."

*   *   *

Javi does not move the way Oscar tells him to and suffers a left jab to his forehead. The punch lands on leather headgear, so Javi is not terribly shaken. Still, he hates the headgear. Told Oscar he wouldn't wear it the first time he was getting ready to spar. Oscar replied fuck off and walked away. They wouldn't let him in the ring without it. So Javi put it on, dipped below the ropes and got the shit kicked out through his ears.

Now he puts it on without saying anything. Still hates the feeling of it, the sag of his eyebrows under its weight. Still can't stand the red leather creeping in on his field of vision, a cherry haze to his left and right. He can barely spit through the mouth gap.

Mostly, though, he remembers Marcel watching him put it on a month or two ago, shaking his head, clucking twice, and asking, "Where'd your pretty face go?"

That had been Marcel's concern from the start.

"Come on in here," he'd said the night they first met on a street in Jackson Heights. "You like my car?"

Javi was leaning over the sidewalk, peering into the Cutlass.

"I got enough. Get inside. Let's move, Mr. Pretty."

Marcel shoved the money into Javi's belt before he'd said a word. Just thrust his hand down the front of his pants, far enough to touch him, though he didn't, and pulled his hand out slowly. Javi looked down to see what was there and what exactly Marcel was so desperate for. He could jump the car and run, take the cash and spend the night waiting for another sedan to sidle up to his concrete step. But Marcel seemed to know he wouldn't, had done something else pushing two hundred into his crotch and then leaving it there.

"I'm good for it, pretty face."

"What do you want?" Javi asked.

"I want you," Marcel said, smiling.

Naked. He'd wanted him naked that first night, and he'd wanted the light on. Marcel drove Javi to his apartment, led him upstairs, and poured them drinks. Sat down on his couch and asked, as if the money were for something else, for Javi to take his shirt off and stand in front of him. Ran his fingers over his stomach and counted all his muscles. Kissed his navel and used his tongue. Pulled his pants off for him.

The next morning Javi got dressed in the dark and didn't notice that Marcel wasn't in bed any longer. He walked out of the bedroom and found the man sitting in a bathrobe at the kitchen table, drinking a cup of coffee.

"Where's your pretty face going? Sit down a while."

Javi stood still and watched as Marcel got up and poured another cup of coffee and placed it down on the table next to his.

"Drink."

Marcel had teeth like a lion, large and white; they were the only thing Javi could see when the man's mouth was open. Javi looked at the front door and his right hand found his pocket. His fingers slipped between the folded twenties inside.

"What's your name, pretty face?" Marcel asked. Then frowning, he added, "I didn't bite last night, so what makes you think I will now?"

Javi walked into the kitchen then and sat down on the chair farthest from Marcel.

"Nombre?" Marcel asked.

"Javier."

"Puerto Rican?

"Dominican."

Marcel nodded. "Both your parents?"

"Yes."

"But you were born in America?"

"Yes," Javi lied, though it didn't feel much like a falsehood anymore. He said yes to anyone who asked, especially strangers, especially the men he barely knew. His mother had taught him to do this.

"Me too," Marcel said, smiling again. He lifted the coffee cup from its saucer and drank. The saucer was spotless. It just barely rang when Marcel set the cup in its depressed center. "Miami, though it's been a while. Have you been to the Dominican?"

"No."

A second lie. Javi had not been back since he was a toddler, but his first four years were in Pedernales, the southernmost border town between the República and Haiti. He remembers houses made of concrete, the walls painted over with murals of the beach, Catholic saints, and the Baton Ballet. He remembers independence day and the street festivals, the pretty girls twirling sticks in their palms.

"Have you ever left the city?"

"No."

A third lie, though perhaps only half of one. He and his family spent a night in Atlantic City on their way north from Baltimore, the place his father managed to wrangle tourist visas for. They went to dinner, spent too much money and could do nothing else but walk around for the rest of the evening. When they got to Queens, his father became a mechanic and his mother worked at an industrial Laundromat. They eventually had some money, but they were always too scared to lose it. They never left the island, let alone the city, and Javi learned to stay put because it was safer, because work was sacred and you never knew how long it was going to last. You got comfortable watching the Mets and eating lemon ice; you wrote home to cousins but made no promises about coming back to visit or bringing them to New York. You had your roots to tend to, baby shoots trying to gash the asphalt of Corona and grab hold of something. And if they couldn't, or if in the end you decided you didn't want them to, that you hated the snow, didn't like the skin of your hands burning from the steam of gargantuan laundry tumblers, then you did like Javi's mom and went back home. You married another man. You left the father and son behind. You wrote them a letter, but you didn't say you were sorry.

"A shame. You'd like it more if you did. You'd know what you were coming back to." Marcel was quiet for a moment, long enough for Javier to ask him a question.

"Why are you up so early?"

"Is this early?" Marcel laughed. "I work in the mornings. Not the nine-to-five shit, but the real morning."

"What do you do?" Javier asked.

"I am the coffee king of Queens!" Marcel said, sitting up. "You ever see those little silver jobs on the street corners? Not the crappy hot dog boxes, but the shiny bullet carts with the Cuban flags on the side? Those are my carts!"

And Javi smiled because Marcel spilled some coffee when he said my carts, his hand jerking the cup in the direction of his heart. Marcel caught himself and wiped some coffee from his bathrobe. He looked up at Javi, and showed him his white teeth again.

"So you own some carts?"

"Thirty-two," Marcel corrected. Javi could see curled hairs poking out through the bathrobe. Maybe two hours ago Javi's head had been on that chest. He would have left as soon as they were done, but in bed and languid, Marcel had pulled Javi in, told him to relax and sleep. Said his bed was comfortable. Said he already had the money. So spend the night. Then he'd pulled Javi's face to his sternum, gathered his hand in his. Javi didn't remember falling asleep.

"Best damn coffee north of Havana," and Marcel took another sip from his cup. "Why don't you try some already?" He grinned and pushed the second cup across the table.

Javi nodded and slipped his finger through the handle. He brought it to his lips, but the coffee was scalding, and he pushed it away quickly, spilling a brown river across the tabletop.

Marcel bellowed. "No damn good if it's cold, Javi! Ha!"

Javi touched his burnt lips and felt the hot skin. He licked the pink flesh with his tongue and tried blowing air on it. Still laughing, Marcel got up from his chair and came over to the boy.

"Go home, bonito. Sleep all day. But then come back here tonight. I need to see my carts. They are like my niños, and I can't spend the whole morning looking at your pretty face."

*　　*　　*

Oscar can see that Javi is not ready for Friday night. He can see how badly his first fight will go, how quickly the other boxer will likely bring him down. He can see Javi's face on the mat. Even now he overreaches, tries to get his right hook into the guy's mouth instead of keeping his feet. Oscar wonders if he should have him take the headgear off for this final round. Let him feel it. Maybe then he will just go away, and maybe then he won't have to tell him to leave.

Thinking that, Oscar feels the same pain in his side he did at the funeral, Javi standing next to him like family and Oscar wanting to push him away. Maybe worse; maybe push him down there with Marcel. The boy had come right up to him, placed himself at his right hand, and Oscar worried that he would reach out to him. Just the two of them and all of Marcel's vendors huddled around a hole in the ground. Stood right fucking next to him, which maybe was better than across the hole since Oscar didn't have to look at him then. Could just watch the vendors, though he couldn't see them all in the fog. But they were quiet, which unnerved him. On the street a person could hear one of Marcel's vendors from around the corner, shouting, which, according to Marcel, was the best way to entice a cold stomach looking for hot coffee. Always in Spanish, too, even though some of the boys were white or black or anything but Latino. Oye! Oye! Café! Café aquí!

"You got to get them excited, Oscarito, or they won't give a damn, they'll keep walking until they get home and can boil their own shit. You got to wave the flag if you want the bull to charge, hermano."

They were faithful to Marcel in that way, shouting whatever it was Muchi told them to. Oscar found the face of the vendor who worked right outside his gym who always had a cup ready for him when he unlocked the doors in the morning. Manny? Miguel? He wasn't sure, but his mouth was shut, and Oscar thought him a different person with his lips pressed together. Where was the flailing tongue? Where was the long, drawn out

Señor Matador? The boy called him that every morning, probably because Muchi had told him to, probably because Marcel thought it was funny: Mr. Killer, the master of future man-matadors. The vendor was a statue right then, chin down low, and Oscar wondered if, as the sole inheritor of maybe thirty-plus silver coffee carts, he could just ask the boy to find another street to hawk his juice on. Go anywhere else; just don't let me hear you around the corner when I come to open up.

In the ring, Javi takes a hard hit to his side and a follow-up hook to his downturned face. He stumbles but then rights himself. He's not scared at least. He doesn't mind being hit. Marcel had said as much the first time he brought Javier to the gym and asked to speak to Oscar alone in the cramped office by the locker room.

"Javi, take a look around. I need to talk to Oscar." He'd grinned at the boy and Javi wandered off toward the ring to watch a sparring match.

In the office Oscar walked behind the bare metal desk he kept for appearances and fell into a wooden rolling chair. Marcel stood by the entrance and stared out through the door glass. Oscar could only imagine him spying on Javier.

"You haven't seen enough of him already?" Oscar asked.

"Silencio, hermano, you just met the boy. What a tongue. And you couldn't shake the boy's hand? I'm sure he's washed it since the last time we touched."

Marcel turned away from the glass and Oscar had to stare at the wall. There was no shaming his brother.

"Oscarito, don't joke, ok? I want your help with Javi."

Marcel had done this before, had called in his favors for a useless boy. "What are you? His fairy godfather?" He'd wanted to sound mean. Maybe like their mother.

"Ha! You bet, but I don't leave at midnight. You should see what I do at midnight."

"Fuck, Muchi, you want me to hire another Tomás?" and Oscar threw his hands on the table.

"Lo siento, I told you that was my fault." Marcel brought two fists to his chest and frowned. "But Javi is no Tomás, and this is what, the second time in how many years I ask something of you? Tomás was a long time ago, man."

"I'm still paying for the equipment. You know how much six speed bags cost? And you knew the kid was shooting shit."

"You gonna fault my big-ass heart? Yeah, Tomás was a fuck-up, but I told you I would pay for all that shit." Even then Marcel reached for his wallet.

Oscar stood, shoving his hand out in front of him and said, "No, Muchi." No, because he was his brother and Tomás had not really been his fault and because Tomás had somehow worked well for a while. The gym had been cleaner and Oscar had been able to go home earlier at nights. He'd been able to lock up at eight without scrubbing down the mats. He'd been able to get dinner at a reasonable hour and fall asleep to the news and not wake up like some battered ship about to run ashore. Everything good, maybe better, until equipment started disappearing. "No" because the gym was not really Oscar's, not yet, not until he paid Muchi back the loan he'd given him, interest free for all goddamn time, the proud-papa look on his older brother's face when they found the right spot, the right corner, the cheap punching bags and a Chilean artist who would do the sign out front for half what the guy in the phonebook wanted.

"Lo siento, Muchi. Of course. Shit, man, of course. He can clean the mats, wash the lockers. Whatever." Oscar then looked out the glass at Javier. He saw the boy bouncing in front of the ring and leaning forward to see better under the ropes. The boy's jeans slid up his calves, and Oscar could see his tendons stretch. "Today? You want him in here today?" Oscar asked.

"Hermano, listen. I want you to work with Javier."

"What?" and Oscar had to pause a moment. "Like you want me to train him?"

"Yessir." Marcel grabbed Oscar's shoulder and squeezed him hard. "Make him one of your boys," and Marcel laughed loud enough to break the door glass. "Make him one of your rippled matadors! Un matador!" his brother said again like a goddamn macaw.

"Forgive me, Muchi, but I don't have a fucking clue why you want me to train your plaything."

Marcel's laughing came to halt and he sighed, looking back out through the door glass. Oscar explored his face, but Marcel kept his eyes out the door.

"I want to keep him, Oscar." Marcel knocked on the glass. "If he mops up sweat, you think he'll stay? He won't. Somebody else will find him, or he'll just leave. He always looks ready to go, you know? Like he hates it here, but doesn't know anything else. He's got some grudge against this town. But you put his name on a locker and give him a pair of gloves, maybe he'll hate it a little less. Maybe he'll train and like it enough to keep coming back to you. And if he stays with you…"

Oscar peered out at Javi and watched the boy.

"And you can tell, Oscarito, I know you can, just by looking at him—he won't be so bad. He won't win anything, but he's quick. He doesn't stand still. He won't lie around in bed with me all day. I've tried. But maybe he could be a lowly on a ticket, just one of the names, no face, you know? Shit, he'll still help you mop up at night, he knows that."

Marcel was right; the boy couldn't stand still. The sparring match was almost over, and the two fighters looked tired, but Javi still followed them around the ring. He even jumped a little when either landed a blow. Then the boy turned toward them and smiled. Marcel lifted his hand and waved. Oscar saw something then in Javi's face, maybe because he smiled and the light landed right on his teeth.

"He fucking looks like you," Oscar said. The straight Roman nose, the high brow, the eyebrows darker than the hair. "I don't mean to be a coño, Muchi, but that's a little weird. You like your own face that much?"

Marcel turned to his brother and grinned.

"Don't be a fool, Oscarito. You know what he looks like—he looks like Miami. He looks like he should be on a beach somewhere. He should be out in the sun. I swear to God, he was born a sea turtle, popped right out of a slick, rubbery shell and swallowed sand first thing. He should be running in the surf with his shirt off. Just running. And who knows? Maybe a little sweat washing over his shoulders."

"All right, all right," Oscar said, turning away from the window and putting his hand up.

But Marcel went on. "Maybe naked in the surf…"

"Basta!" and Oscar was laughing.

"Si, hermano," Marcel said, his teeth showing.

Oscar sat down on the edge of his desk and scratched the skin beneath his beard.

"So what? You want to turn New York into Miami? First the coffee carts and now the boy? You gonna build a beach on the Hudson next? Maybe plant some red mangroves in Kissena? Is Javier even from Florida?"

"It don't matter, man. That's what he looks like. That's enough. Like a little bit of sea spray instead of the ocean. Not that dark shit running under Throgs Neck, you know? I'm talking about the waves off North Shore. All I want are a few drops, hermano. Can you help me out, mi Oscarito?"

Oscar could see Marcel smiling at him and could count the teeth like marble stones in his mouth, but he could also hear the baritone tremble in his brother's words. He could hear the plea in his voice, the same shaky tone that came out of Marcel when he asked, "Como está, Mamá?"

He nodded slowly, "Of course, Muchi."

*   *   *

There is only a minute or so left in the match, Javi is certain, but he has never sparred for this long before, a full extra round three days before his first fight. He wonders if Oscar is still watching him or if he has gone to check his books or instruct the other fighters, or maybe even inspect the equipment. Oscar has been circling the gym nonstop since Marcel's shooting ten days ago. It's still not clear what happened. Gunshots and two bodies: one, Marcel's; the other, one of his coffee vendors. Javi thinks the not knowing is Oscar's reason for pacing his mats. The man stands still long enough and the whole world hits him. Better to keep moving. Better to keep ducking the punch. Which is all Javi can manage to do right now. He long ago gave up trying to beat his partner, a better fighter than Javi, which had been Oscar's intent.

"You won't learn anything stepping on chickadees," he told Javi this morning. "Got to peck a rooster if you want to take down the henhouse."

Bob and weave, duck and block, bob and weave— like a sinking ship that won't make up its mind, Javi thinks, and he tries a left jab. But he doesn't cover up, and his partner finds his ribcage, puts a hurt on his lung. Javi damn near spits out his mouth guard, but grits his teeth instead. He finds a rope and does his best not to fall over. It will throb tomorrow and probably Thursday as well. It will be hard to breath without grabbing his side. The skin will bruise and he will see it in the mirror. He will come back to this moment in the morning.

If Marcel could still talk, there would be a way to forget about it. There would be a cold pack next to Javi on the couch. There would be saucers waiting for shots of espresso on the coffee table in the living room. There would be Bebo Valdés on the tape player whipping along some ancient big band. There would be Marcel in the cocina mincing pork with spice and lard, rolling the mixture into silk-thin dough, and shoving the empanadas into the oven for twenty minutes, those minutes spent checking and touching Javi's bruise, circling it with a cube of ice.

"What did Oscar say?" Marcel asked once after finding a bruise the size of a grapefruit on Javi's left bicep.

"Nothing. He flicked it actually. Maybe said something about stretching the arm before icing it."

"He said nothing else? Just ice?"

"And stretching. He isn't like you. He doesn't come running when I stub my toe. He's got other fighters, you know? He can't watch over Muchi's boy all day long."

"He flicked you in the arm? Like this?" and Marcel poked him where it hurt. Javi jumped, but Marcel pushed him back down onto the couch. He struggled, but Marcel had him by the shoulder.

"Hombre here needs to toughen up. No wonder Oscar didn't say anything—didn't want to muss your feathers. Probably thought you would break if he did."

"I knocked the other guy on his ass!" Javi almost screamed. He struggled but knew Marcel wouldn't let him up. "You should see his face! My arm got nothing on his face!"

Marcel squeezed Javi's shoulder hard and his grin went away. Javi could feel Marcel's big fingers dig into his muscles, could sense tenderness in the way they pressed into his skin without hurting him.

"I am only concerned with your face, pretty boy," and Marcel put his other hand in Javi's still damp hair and combed it to the side with his fingers. "Don't let them fuck with this face." he looked over Javi's face, and after a moment asked, "You really liking the boxing?"

"It's all right."

Marcel pinched his ear and went into the kitchen to check the empanadas. On the couch Javi massaged the skin around his bruise and listened as Marcel slid the baking tray out of the oven. There would be four empanadas, two for each of them, but Marcel would only eat one and then force Javi to take the other three. Protein for el matador.

From the kitchen, "Oscar tells me you're quick."

"He tells me I dance in the ring."

"So? Ali would float like a fucking insect—why can't you dance?"

"It wastes energy."

"What does he want you to do? Stand still and get hit?"

"He says bounce from foot to foot, not side to side."

Marcel walked out of the kitchen with the empanadas on a plate with two forks. He gave the plate to Javi and sat down on the coffee table across from him. He watched Javi spear the first empanada.

"Oscar knows what he's telling you," Marcel said. "He ended careers when he was your age."

"I know, I know. I just don't like standing still. Why not move till the other guy gets tired and then get in his face? Everyone there knows they can beat me, so why not let them chase me for a little bit?"

Marcel smiled, but just barely. He took the plate from Javi and cut a corner off of the second empanada with the edge of his fork. Bringing the crust to his mouth, Marcel looked at Javi and asked him, "You thinking of quitting on Oscar?"

Javi watched him chew, his lips pressed tight, no crumbs around his mouth, no flakes catching in his stubble. Javi liked it when Marcel ate because it was the only time he was quiet. It was a different face from when Marcel chattered, and Javi thought his eyes stood out when his teeth were hidden. Big and brown and slow moving, as if they already knew what they were going to see, so there was no rush in seeing it. Javi knew what Marcel was asking, even so much younger than the well-kept coffee entrepreneur, even tired, hungry for more meat pies and sweat still darkening the fabric of his t-shirt.

"No, I will not give up on Oscar," Javi said, and Marcel's brown eyes moved just a tiny bit. "Not yet." And when Marcel started to grin, "He is too good of a coach."

"All right," Marcel said, nodding. He smiled slow and showed his teeth. He licked them bare. Javi thought, and now he will kiss me. But Marcel just handed him the plate of empanadas.

The indifferent gesture reminded Javi of his father. He'd not gone after his wife when she ran off, perhaps too afraid he'd never make it back to the States or the shitty garage he co-ran with another Dominican up on Willet's Point. More likely he'd begun to believe all the things he'd spent over a decade telling Javi: This is where we live now. This home. There's no going back. There's nothing back there but being broke and dying early. He wasn't as vocal, though, after Javi's mother was gone; he just worked longer days, filled the hours he used to spend with her with oil changes, rickety suspensions and loose ball bearings. He got over the empty space in his bed by never touching it, by sleeping five hours a night and always facing the window in the bedroom. He took her departure as a fact of life, something to adjust to but never look back on. Drank it down like a cup of cold coffee.

"Finish these," Marcel said. "I need some café."

He was gruff like his father, too, and louder. Wouldn't just say what he wanted but would act it out like the goddamn Verbena de Navidad; a bunch of theatrics and histrionic bullshit to soften the demands. Javi knew Marcel was like that with everyone. His father rarely asked for anything. It made Javi think he had something on the guy, or would have had something, if he'd been willing to speak up. He remembered how long it took the man to ask him where he went all night, why he wasn't pulling longer hours at the shop. He was eighteen then, done with school and supposedly a grown-ass human. His father wanted to know where Javi was getting his money from. His hands, his father said, were real pretty, and by this of course he meant two things. Javi wondered how much he'd figured out, how long it took him to really see, and whether or not he would have ever said something outright. Probably not, and the fact made Javi's head hurt, because it meant when he left, when he stopped going home, sick as he was of his father's tired looks, his crumpled hands and gasoline smell, Javi still wanted him to more than not.

Javi wondered also what Oscar had been telling Marcel. He and Oscar didn't talk much at the gym after workouts, when they swept the floors side by side or wiped down the leather ropes of the ring, one following the other like a shadow around the platform. During training Oscar only spoke of what pertained to boxing, and even that was limited to the moment: "Step with your front foot;" "Drop your left and cover your ribs;" "Jump over the goddamn rope! Don't just step over it."

Never anything about the next day or when the next sparring session would be or what Oscar saw for Javi down the line. Nothing about Javi as a future fighter.

Maybe Oscar had seen something in Javi's restless feet. Maybe he'd said something to Marcel in his back office about Javi being some cagey fighter who looked as though he could jump the ropes any second. Those things were true, and if Oscar had said them to Javi's face he would not have denied them. He was restless. He did have some itch to move, some feeling of flight working his legs every day. He'd gotten tired of Queens, its streets, its bitter winter and men. He'd gotten sick of cologne and condoms, of dirty sedans and hourly rates. He'd gotten sad with walking home in the dark with a small weight in his pocket that seemed to pull him closer to the pavement. He hated knowing how many blocks he was from his father's shop, how many extra miles he'd walked to go around Xenia Street in Corona just to avoid seeing the bent over man. Something like seven years since Javi had last lain eyes on his father. Just the same, he had no grander plans, only a small box of endless twenties he kept in a bureau in his studio apartment. Just the cash and the foolish notion that somewhere else might be bigger, fuller than New York. Javi knew Marcel was teaching him how to stay, tethering him to a stubborn heart.

"Marcel," he called lightly.

"What, pretty face?"

"How come you left Miami?"

Marcel came in from the kitchen with a pair of clean white coffee cups on saucers.

"What?"

"Why did you leave Miami?

Marcel slid one coffee cup onto the table and took the other one with him to the tan armchair across from the couch. He sat down slowly, and then made a show of blowing away the steam rising from his cup. He looked at Javier.

"Because," he said, "it was too hot."

"Bullshit."

"Ha! You don't believe me? You've never been in the swamplands of Hialeah come August, man. You do your little jog around the ring and pretend you know what sweat is, but you don't have a goddamn clue."

"Fuck you. I don't see thousands of cubanos running north for the snow."

Holding his cup and saucer in one hand, Marcel brought his hand to his face and rubbed his chin. He touched his cheekbone and rubbed the tender spot just below his left eye.

"No joke," Javi said.

"Oye, Javi, it was too hot. You misunderstand me."

A pause. "It was so damn hot you couldn't get close to a body."

Javi waited only a moment before asking, "Whose body?"

"Just a boy's," Marcel said waving his hand across his face as if dusting for flies. "Just a boy from school."

"Did he break your heart?" Javi asked, and he was surprised by how sincere he sounded, by how much he wanted to know.

"No, Javi. But his older brothers damn near broke my face."

A blank moment passed, and after it Javi could only think about how he had never taken care of another person beside himself. He could only think about how young he was, how much older beautiful Marcel was.

"Then my mother knew. She was angry."

Marcel sipped his drink.

"Your people católico?" he asked.

"My father was, but then he started working Sundays."

"Mi mamá is a diehard, though she's not into the saints or anything. She only prays to the one true God, you know? And she knows the Latin. Didn't take to that Second Council stuff and swore she'd never learn the Mass in English, though that's just cause she's terrible at English. The day after I told her about the boy and his brothers, she locked herself in her bedroom and spent six hours praying. She did that every day for three months. Three months! She was praying for my recovery, that Christo would come down and clean me up. Clap me on the head and send me straight."

Javi imagined his father crossing himself in front of the picture of Jesus he'd hung in the office of his garage.

"But then I walk by her room one day and I realize she's not praying to God or Christ or the Holy Ghost. She's praying to my father. She's calling out to Ramón, begging him to come back and fix his faggot son."

Marcel swallowed more coffee and steam lifted over his eyes.

"When people are pissed, Javier, when they can't let go of things, the air around them—it heats up. Hialeah was already a burning suburb, but after hearing her whisper Papi's name in the dark—Ramón, Ramón, Ramón—it was just too damn hot."

Falling asleep beside Marcel hours later, Javi thought of the word "exile," of a man driven out. Driven north by the heat. Long after Marcel's chest found a sturdy rhythm, Javi lay awake wondering if he was weak. The city was both hot and cold, and what had he gotten that he hadn't asked for? He'd given himself out for years, and somehow he'd gotten Marcel. Javi pushed his face into the big man's back and breathed in his luck.

But now, his head on fire and locked inside a leather headpiece, Javi wonders if he is wasting his legs inside the ring. His reason to stay in the city bled out on the street ten days ago, and isn't that why people leave the places they're from? Because they eventually know everything about them? Because they know how hot August is, who has lived on what corner, who has died in what gutter? His being gone is a force, Javi thinks, his tired hands barely covering his face. The other man still swings, but he doesn't care. Javi doesn't want to dance anymore. He wants to run.

*   *   *

Oscar is talking to a boy younger than Javi when he hears the final ping that ends the sparring match. The boy he talks to is sixteen, and he wants to join the gym. He is a fast talker, but polite, and Oscar asks him if he has ever been in a fight. The boy starts to tell a story about some battle in the schoolyard, two older kids ganging up on him, but Oscar cuts him off. He tells him to go home, that boxing is not a sport, and then heads toward the ring.

Why not now, he thinks while watching Javi stumble into his corner. Just take the boy into his office and tell him that his first fight will be his last. How hard?

Much too hard. Javi has collapsed onto his stool and pants like a madman. He already looks broken, and Oscar does not want to kill the boy. Instead he approaches the ring like it's any other Tuesday and leans against the bottom rope.

"Good," he says. "You can still walk. All we can hope for."

Javi nods but is tired and lets his chin drop to the side. Oscar envisions a pigeon tucking its beak under its wing.

"Did Bruno tag you?" he asks.

Javi turns his body and lifts up his left arm. Oscar can see swelling in the skin and the red mark of a well-placed inside hook.

"Take a deep breath," he tells the boy.

Javi's chest expands.

"Does it hurt?"

He shakes his head.

"Bien."

Javi spits his mouth guard out onto the mat. He still has his gloves on and when he looks at them, Oscar steps closer.

"Here."

The boy lifts his gloves and Oscar gets at the Velcro straps. Javi holds his arms rigid as the mitts slide off. As soon as his hands are free, he goes for his headgear.

The chinstrap quickly loosened, the whole outfit comes down. The boy scratches his head and wipes sweat from his eyes.

"How you feel?" Oscar asks him.

Javi shrugs and Oscar thinks it might be dangerous to let him fight. He might get angry in the ring, angry at the world and try to take it out on the other guy. Or worse, he might fall away, show up seeming drunk but really just gone, and get beat to hell on Friday night.

"I'm okay," and Javi throws out a couple of quick jabs to prove it. Oscar sighs. No such luck in this world.

Fine, Oscar thinks, but I don't want to see him.

"Javi, do everything the same tomorrow except the running, and do it all at home. You should start clearing your head for Friday. Let things be a little different, but don't fuck the routine. Then, on Thursday, don't do shit. Sleep in. Go to a bar at noon. Drink a beer. Then go home. Stretch. Go to bed. Done. Then fight night. Claro?"

"Okay," the boy says, but Oscar can hear the doubt in his voice.

"For a first fight you need all your legs, okay?"

Javi nods and Oscar watches the logic wash over him.

"Friday at six," he says, and he thinks it is enough to walk away.

"Oscar…"

"Yeah?"

"Did they call you? Did they find the guy?"

Oscar doesn't have to lie.

"Not yet."

*   *   *

It has been twelve nights of sleeping alone, and Javi wonders if that is what his walking says, if that is why a car has pulled up to the curb just ahead of him. He is going home drunk from a bar not far from his gray apartment. At noon he went in and ordered a beer. He drank it, then meant to order a sandwich, but purchased another drink instead. Javi does not like beer much but will do whatever Oscar tells him to. Drink a beer, Javi. Go home. Stretch. He did not say drink four beers, but Javi felt an easy sleep following the second. Three. Four. Go home and stretch, Javi mumbles to himself. Push your hands out over your head; draw out the ribcage. Javi can feel the shot to his side from two days ago. There is a fight tomorrow. Javi wonders if he will go to it.

Left, right, left, right, Javi passes by the pulled over car, a blue sedan with the engine running, and does not look through the window. If he doesn't look the person will likely go haunt some other lost-looking boy. There are rules. Javi can hear the passenger window coming down.

"Hey, guy, can I give you a lift?"

The kindness of strangers is something other than kindness on this street, and Javi maybe should have gone home a different way, picked a sidewalk with more storefronts or light posts.

"It's warm in here," says the voice.

Javi stops next to the front bumper, and when he does, the car pulls forward. A man leans over the console and looks up at him.

"Where you headed?"

"What do you want?" Javi asks.

The man leans back and appears put off. His eyes narrow and his mouth tightens at the corners. He's older than Javi and has bits of gray in his hair. He wears a nice jacket, a white collar poking out around the neck. Javi checks his hands and sees well-kept cuticles, clean fingernails. He is attractive, and that puts Javi at ease. He never got into cars with ugly men.

"Can we talk in the car?" the man asks.

Here Javi truly misses Marcel's voice. Not the sound of it, but the certainty in almost everything he said. This guy in the car wants to barter with Javi, wants to drive in circles around the block and see what they can work out. He wants to spend some time with a boyish young man in a room somewhere. Or maybe just in this car in an empty lot. So many places in this city where streetlights don't reach. It's only ever a matter of finding someone. The rest is waiting. He can't always do this.

The man leans forward again and this time reaches all the way over to the passenger side. He unlocks the door and then opens it. He can't reach too far past the seat and the door only swings an inch or two away from the car. But it's open now, and the man is trying.

"It won't take long," he says, and this time he flashes an easy smile.

These older men, Javi thinks—he never asked Marcel why. He didn't want to know how many there were before him, always scared of the possibility that he'd given himself over too easily. The possibility of an end point, of some day coming when beautiful Marcel wouldn't grin and there'd be the door. Javi didn't want to hang that question over their bed in case it wasn't really a matter of love.

There's the possibility of this man putting his clean fingers in Javi's hair. There's the possibility he'll take Javi to his apartment and into his bedroom. There's a chance it'll be nice and the bed will be big and it will feel like something he once had. So Javi pulls open the car door and slides into the passenger seat.

Javi thinks to ask his name before they start talking, before they set the terms. What can I call you? But he doesn't, because he knows it's against the rules.

*   *   *

The radio is on, but Oscar cannot enjoy it because of the papers littering his kitchen table. No stacks of anything, just two or three layers of legal documents relating to Oscar's inheritance and newfound ownership of a small Queens-area coffee vending outfit. Also the leasing information for Marcel's apartment and a list of furniture. Then the statement of liquid assets and the will, which is brief, Marcel's whole world bequeathed to Oscar. At the bottom of the final page, Marcel's penmanship is grand and wavy, and Oscar thinks his signature is as loud as any sound he ever made. More than half of it spills past the line.

There are the specifics of the business as well. Things like inventory and supplies, distribution of beans and sugar packets, a million thin red coffee stirrers. Vendors have called him asking for these things and other information. Requests to move location, crass demands for a raise, hints at work-supplied glove wear, and even one demand for a two-week in memoriam vacation. To Marcel! El jéfe!

Oscar wants only to be a gym owner and a trainer. Wants only to think about the fights this weekend. Wants to listen to his goddamn radio and drink his goddamn coffee with rum. Wants more than anything to stop having dreams about big teeth and roosters crowing. They wake him up and make him thirsty; to go back to sleep he has to open his one bedroom window and hope for the sounds of traffic, the voices of pedestrians four floors down bouncing off the asphalt.

On the table he also has his scorecard. It is nothing official, just the little index card he turns vertical come Friday and on which he lists his fighters. Tomorrow morning he'll put all their names on the card along with their opponents and then he'll star the winners. At the fights he will make notes beneath the names, one word chicken scratches about areas for improvement, things done wrong, little flaws he will expose on Monday.

The first fight is Javi's, and Oscar stops when he sees the kid's name. This has less to do with Marcel than with the timing of things. This is the boy's first fight, the clash he's trained two months for. This is the week the boy really decides on being a boxer. It's something to be excited about. But how can anyone expect anything but failure? Marcel is dead. What's Javi going to do in the ring? Steady his legs and swing? He won't bounce now, Oscar thinks. Those tendons gone flaccid—stones in his shoes, boulders in his pockets. He's going to get beat. He's going to get thrown, and he doesn't have a chance.

What a horrible kind of hurt. Oscar feels for the boy, wants to pour a stiff drink in his honor and put up a headstone for his stillborn future. And he knows, sadly, that even with the common thread of Marcel, the life around which he and Javi have circled for two short months, that this is the closest he's ever felt to the boy. He is going to lose something very soon, and Oscar knows how that goes down.

Oscar knows how easily a hand breaks, how the wrong angle really fucks things up. He was winning at the time; he'd twice knocked Salitas to the mat and was working on a third descent. One more and TKO; one more and vict-o-ree. But he caught the guy's elbow straight on. He'd pushed his knuckles into the sharp edge of Salitas' funny bone and a couple of things cracked. He played through the round, but they called it quick when his trainer touched his mitt and he screamed his mouth guard right past his lips. The swelling hurt the most, and they had to cut his glove off in the end. He couldn't uncurl his fisted fingers.

Some things you can't come back from, and, therefore, some things you can't go back to. Not the same right hook. Not the same bones and muscle. New metacarpals that could turn to dust if he hit someone the same way just one more time.

And then back home with Mamá. Looking for some job. Looking for a way to make Hialeah somewhere else besides where he learned to box. On the phone with Marcel and nothing to say because his brother was up north and sounded happy.

"What are you gonna do now, man?" Marcel asked. Oscar thought there was a bit of joy in his brother's question, like the opportunity had finally come, the time when he could draw him away from damp Miami and up north to the city. Oscar had the sense that Marcel was smiling on the other end of the line. He'd prayed for this somehow, and Díos had listened.

"I can't leave her now," Oscar told him. "With the boxing, I would have had to go now and then, but what? I'm going to just head out for good?"

"Oscarito, I've got a place for you."

"I don't need an apartment," Oscar said.

"I'm not talking about a place for you to put your shit, man. There's an empty gym that would look something special with our last name on it."

Talk about the sweet sound of the devil's tongue. He argued with Marcel for the rest of the phone call and for the weeks that followed, but he knew in his heart and in his dormant forearms that nothing would make him happier than finding again the purpose-filled scent of sweat and leather. Fucking Muchi. Oscar wanted to ask Marcel And who's left after me, but what for? Marcel was already the estranged son and not by choice, or at least the choice had been impossible: suffer your mother's voice calling out the ghost of your dead father or find a new home. What Marcel didn't hear, what Oscar had never told him, was the way Mamá sometimes cursed their father's name during her brutal incantations, a blasphemy she began only after Muchi headed to New York. Through the walls Oscar could hear her shift from something like earnest supplication to painful accusation: Your son, Ramón, your son you left behind. Once, just once and almost a year later, he banged on the walls to make her stop. Agueda stayed in her room the rest of that day, but the next morning she came into the kitchen, red-eyed and weak, and pushed herself into Oscar's arms. He told her that she had to stop; if she didn't, he'd have to leave to stay sane.

Agueda said, "Maybe you should leave anyway. This house is cursed."

"Are you trying to drive us all out?" he asked.

It was the only time Oscar could remember that he'd said something, halfhearted as it was, in defense of his brother. He'd expected his mother to slap him, but instead she cried into his shirtsleeves.

"You can call him," Oscar said.

"I can't," his mother said.

In the end, those were the words that Oscar borrowed, the words that allowed him to leave for New York: he loved his mother but couldn't stay; I want to, but I can't. So he told her I'll be back soon, Mamá! ¡No pasa nada! Agueda had some tears about his going, but she didn't hold him back. He was the only cariño left, so what could she say? How alone in her faith and widowhood did she want to be? They were a family adrift; each of them swam alongside one another, but each of them had to account for their own air.

Eventually it was like Oscar hadn't lost anything. Mamá was always by the phone and there was a gym. There were hitting bags and weights and a square platform with ropes going round in threes. And Marcel—what a face! As though the gym were a gift to himself, the final bit to his New York paraíso. He watched Oscar walk around the floor space like a child who'd found God. Oscar knew it would be different, knew the punches wouldn't be his, but hell, how much closer did a man need to be? He could drink the sweat of his fighters and be full.

And always the truth to come back to: Marcel the guardian angel, el jéfe and San Nicolas. Plucked Oscar from hot Miami and carried him to New York on a beautiful promise. There were nights Oscar fell asleep blessing his brother's name, because who else would have given him boxing back?

On the kitchen table, Oscar's scorecard is still mostly white, and he now picks it up. He thinks of the joy in this little thing. He thinks of how the card makes his weekend, gives him a Monday to envision, a particular space to go back to. But pobre Javi! His Marcel is just as gone as Oscar's brother. Oscar does not really know that Marcel and never much wanted to, but he was there just the same, and he was, for better or worse, that's boy's lover. Oscar is afforded the man's things, but what can Javi drag home with him? And it pains him to think it, but not even Marcel's bed to crawl into. Not even the sheets they shared. The boy will crumble in the ring tomorrow night, and there will be no one calling his name from the crowd.

The phone rings, and Oscar knocks a set of papers off the table in response. He quickly puts the score card into his breast pocket and moves to answer the call. He picks up after the third ring.

"Hello?" Oscar touches his face. He fingers a button on his shirt. "Yes, I'm his brother."

*   *   *

Even though Javi hasn't left the city limits in twenty years, he realizes at this moment how round the whole damn world is. He understands that if he got on a bus and headed to California and then took a plane to another country and just kept going that this is where he would end up. He'd come right back to this blue car, one big lap around the globe, giant steps going nowhere.

The man in the car has offered him forty dollars to do nothing. He wants Javi to sit back and pull down his pants. He wants to suck Javi's dick. The rooster come home to roost, because this is how Javi got into this shit. This man might as well have been the first gray-haired customer to approach him with a trick and an offer. Javi was seventeen and at a bar in South Jamaica, dancing with boys he knew from high school. People handing him drinks, and friends groping his ass. A well-dressed stranger found him on the dance floor and wasn't pushy. Was just laughing and having a good time like the rest of them. Then the cursory touches, the nice hands that poked at Javi's lower back, his neck, his ribs, his crotch. The man saying something about a car and Javi nodding because he was good looking, because the stranger could move on the parquet. The fact that the man didn't want to kiss him in the car. The quickness with which he had Javi on his back and reeling. The man's experienced tongue. For whatever reason, twenty dollars in Javi's hand when things were finished, when he would have let the man do just the same for free and thanked him in the end.

Javi loved it at first. Men everywhere who would get him off and pay for the pleasure, better, easier work than jalopy cars on a lift and rusted-out pickups wanting for grease. The fact that he enjoyed it blurred the line just enough, made him forget about his father, that old man's look. This was for fun. This was goofing on Saturday night, a real good time. What was the money for? For his having to walk out to a car or go for a ride or spend a night in a hotel room. A relocation fee.

The only difference is how this guy struggles to keep Javi hard. Javi knows it might be his thing, the kind of week he's had, but he wants to put it on the man's mouth and not his mindset. What a thought, him not being able to get it up! What a gutter he'd be in then, alone and limp. The man grunts and Javi knows he should at least make a noise. He should writhe if he wants his forty. Javi feels the man cup his balls, and he sighs, because as pretty as this man's hands are, they can't do shit for him.

Javi should be grateful, and he knows this. Almost twenty-five and still cars pull up to him. There are so many younger ones than he—shit, is he really still a boy? The size of Marcel's chest made Javi feel young and delicate again. Made him feel like New York was the same city he'd started turning in, open and wide, men knocking down doors to see him with his shirt off. What had the months before Marcel been like? Thinner and leaner. His stubble came in quicker. His pubic hair wasn't as soft. When he was tired, it showed, petite bird feet stepping into the corners of his eyes.

Javi looks down the stranger's back and sees the bulge of his wallet in his pant's pocket. There had been a time when he could demand seventy-five, even a hundred, and pepper-headed customers would say yes without blinking. Javi isn't sure he can argue anymore. He'd not even tried with this one, the man's eyes lighting up when Javi agreed to so little.

"Slower," he tells the stranger, and the man adjusts his pace.

That's what felt good, Javi thinks. The control. They have the money, but that isn't what gets Javi hard. He likes telling them what to do.

"Use your tongue more…yeah. Just like that."

The sound of the man in his lap is like an echo underwater, all slow and distorted. His little movements and wet lips. His tiny smacks. This is how it works. This is how Javi moves from one day to the next. Yet nothing happens. Javi's penis gets wetter, and he can feel a slick liquid run down into his boxers, but he's not any more aroused. His beautiful, boyish dick is asleep and won't wake up.

Javi knows then that he won't come, and thinks of maybe just telling the guy. He wonders if this is what's to be. He will get older and fewer men will pull up to the curb with a bulging crotch and a handful of folded bills fresh from an ATM. The ones that do will fail to satisfy him, and it will be his fault as much as theirs. Or maybe this is Marcel's fault, his love upsetting what Javi knew of men and fucking; Marcel's love having spoiled Javi's fun, really his work he reminds himself, his rounds on Saturday night, as if it was his body, his young self, not Marcel, now laid to rest.

But then he feels a finger slip from his scrotum and start messing with his anus, and he squirms. He throws his own hand into the mess and slaps the finger away. The man shoots up and damn near clips Javi's chin with the back of his head.

"What the fuck is your problem?" he says.

"Just don't do that," Javi shoots back, and he's already pulling up his pants.

"Where the hell are you going?"

"I don't think—"

But the man hits Javi hard before he can apologize. Not a punch, but more than a slap. An open handed strike to the side of Javi's head with the meat of his palm. Javi covers up for what comes next, and thankfully, the man can't get any leverage, just pummels Javi's held up forearms with a series of angry blows. The first one stuck, though, and Javi wonders if there will be a bruise next to his left eye in the morning. As he finds the door latch and pushes his way out of the car, the man grabs for him, and Javi has to kick to get out. And then he's on his feet and jogging. Not running, because he knows the guy's not going to bother coming for him. Didn't pay him anyway. Still got his forty and the whole night left to find another boy.

Javi rounds the first corner and looks for a street with traffic on it. He stops jogging and lets himself walk. He's sober now and wide awake, but walks a little funny and thinks the punch has made him dizzy. He touches the skin above his cheekbone and it is hot. There's blood moving in and he doesn't have to wonder. He knows it will turn green and purple and navy blue.

Javi laughs, hears his sound bounce down the street, and thinks of Marcel's question, "You really liking the boxing?" Yes, after a while. Oscar had grown on him. But from the start? No, just the idea of getting smashed in, his nose getting pushed to the side, and his blue eyes swelling shut, the shore encroaching in on the sea. The idea of Marcel seeing him ugly, of having to kiss his bruised cheekbones and cut forehead. The fact of Marcel having to prove his love.

Javi pushes his fingers into the swelling skin and the pain is a starburst. Where did your pretty face go, cariño? Aquí, Muchi. Right here.

* * *

Oscar gets off the phone with the detective assigned to Marcel's homicide and sits back down at the kitchen table. He doesn't touch the card in his pocket or the papers in front of him. He looks around the kitchen. It's gotten dark outside and Oscar should turn on a light.

He doesn't know how to use his hands. They rest palms up in his lap, and Oscar is not familiar with having them open and empty. There's always the card or at least a pencil in one of them, and when he's coaching they curl like the fists he used to make but can't anymore. Always gripping something, even if it's only air.

The same hands, Oscar thinks, and he turns them over in his lap. His nails are short, bitten in spots, and each ring finger is as long as the middle digit next to it. He thinks of his lazy fighters, the ones who come in some days and claim to have empty legs and stone elbows. Same body as yesterday, he tells them, and he leaves it at that. Two, maybe three weeks and they are gone.

The detective had been brief: money missing from the cart and Marcel's wallet stretched wide like a gutted fish next to his body on the sidewalk. A small struggle. Footprints in the snow that led the detective to believe Marcel was running toward the cart when it all happened. Just the front part of his soles pressing into the iced pavement. Running on his toes, Oscar thought, praising Marcel for his footwork—good fighters never let their heels touch the mat. Then the catch: a suspect in custody. An addict with a revolver. Hungry for stuff but needing some cash. A familiar name: Tomás Salazar.

Oscar kicks the table; the papers fan out like a pigeon's wing but do not slip over the edge. It's all the rage he has. He's too damn tired to knock the furniture over or tear up his brother's will. The how and the who have failed to answer the why, and Oscar knows his chance for understanding this pain has escaped. Gone like a career and his heart, the mangled remains that will never function the same. It seems that no one has ever watched over Muchi, and Oscar traces the bones on the back of his right hand with his left thumb.

"Tell me You love him," he says.

Running his hand through his beard, Oscar's forearm brushes against the tip of the card in his pocket. He promised Javi he would tell him as soon as he knew. He could call him now, the night before his first fight. If Javi is doing what Oscar told him to, then he is sleeping. He would wake to the shrill bell of his apartment phone instead of an alarm clock. He'd never make it to his first fight, Oscar thinks.

But won't that be easier? If Oscar tells the boy everything, even who held the gun, then Javi will have a new image of el jéfe in his mind. Murdered by an ex-lover, Marcel will become any other man, and how could Javi avoid suspicion? Then, Oscar is certain, the boy will go. He won't have to ask him to leave. He won't have to explain his absence from the gym. Oscar will stop having the dreams and Marcel will be in heaven where he belongs and he will watch over Oscar but not trouble him. He will keep the gym safe and protect what's left of his little brother's paraíso.

But then Oscar sees the boy's face in his head, the straight Roman nose, the high brow, the eyebrows darker than the hair. His dreams have worked their way into his waking hours. Oscar shuts his eyes, but Javi's face is there as well, and against the black backdrop, the skin goes red, and there is a swollen cheek and a cut lip. Oscar can't decide if what he sees is Javi tomorrow night or Marcel years ago, but the face is gruesome and it remains.

These visions are the greater part of Oscar's inheritance. He wants so badly to give them to Javi, but perhaps there are too many? Perhaps Marcel's death is too big for a broken boy and a washed up corner man. It will likely consume Javi, and then who will it burn through? Oscar does not think he can stand the heat, the flame he thinks will be if he holds the broken face and these dreams for much longer. And is it fair to the boy who will get nothing of Marcel's but quiet mornings from now until another love? But Oscar knows there is no love like Marcel, and Javi is probably already on fire. Fuck, Oscar feels hot under the arms.

How short the days in January and how hot the heater runs in his small apartment. Steam and condensation cloud the windowpane. Oscar shuts his eyes tight and tries to push out the face, but the apparition is resolute, and he realizes how terrifying the face really is—a silent Marcel with a busted jaw shut tight.

Oscar makes a fist and hooks it into the wall, knocks loose a calendar next to the fridge. It is too hot. He and the boy do not deserve this. No, Oscar thinks. It is not fair.

*   *   *

There is a joke going around the small arena when Oscar arrives that Javi was shadow boxing at home and managed to catch himself. Oscar doesn't know what that means but heads for the locker room after checking in with the officials and making sure his other trainers are there. There's no crowd just yet, won't be for Javi's amateur bout which runs first, and so Oscar can hear his footsteps echo in the bleachers set up around the ring. All the lights are on, and Oscar can feel how the lamps heat the stage.

At the rear of the arena he enters a narrow hallway. There are the sounds of water running and men laughing, and Oscar keeps moving till he finds the right door. When he enters, there are only a few men inside: the opponent and his trainers on one side of the dingy room, and Javi sitting upright on a bench opposite the group. And because the arena is nothing much, there's only a sink and a toilet to the right, not even a shower. Maybe fifteen feet between fighters. Oscar waves to Javi's opponent who does not stop talking when he sees him, but nods back, so Oscar moves on to his man. Javi stares directly at him as he nears, and Oscar sees that there's some dark patch near his left eye. Javi is in his match trunks and has had his hands taped, by whom Oscar has no idea. There's a layer of sweat on his face and his shoulders lift generously when he breathes. Javi has been warming up.

"Oye," Oscar says. "Your eye."

Javi brings up his left hand and pokes the blackened skin.

"It's all right. It doesn't really hurt. I can still see to my left."

"How?"

But the boy waves his hand in front of his face, a gesture Oscar's seen before in his brother. Marcel's answer for life's problems; just clear out the flies, brush off the dust. "Let me see," Oscar says, but Javi leans backs when Oscar tries to get close.

The boy snaps at him, "Leave it."

There's a shuffling from the other side of the room, and Oscar hears the other boxer and his trainers leave. A touchy fighter is contagious.

"What happened?" Oscar asks again, this time a little softer, almost a whisper.

"They must have called you," Javi says, and Oscar is unsettled. There's some heat coming off the kid, and Oscar thinks of the face in his dreams, the little blue flame that might rage in his chest.

"After," he says.

"Now."

"His car was pulled up to the curb," Oscar starts. "The driver's side door was open. They took the money from the cart and whatever was in his wallet. They just wanted the money."

"Why was the car door open?" Javi asks.

Oscar hesitates. The detective's story already feels stale in his mouth.

"Marcel was running from the car to the cart."

"To the cart?" Javi asks.

"Yes."

The boy exhales. "What else? Did they arrest someone?"

"Yes."

"Who?"

"A drug addict who had a gun and wanted the money."

"What's his name?"

Looking at his cub fighter, Oscar feels a different sort of pity, one he holds for himself as well as Javi. The bullet doesn't go back into the gun if Oscar tells the boy who Tomás is, was, and Oscar's not sure what else the truth will do besides ruin him. He doesn't want to find out. For the boy's sake, he thinks, and because Oscar doesn't want Javi's face in his dreams for the rest of his life.

"Salazar," he says, leaving the first name alone, letting it wander off unspoken.

Javi's chest starts to move, and his back bucks against the metal locker. The boy's eyes are still closed and his lips are pressed tight. The look on his face could be pain or pleasure, but whatever it is, it's throwing Javi against the wall. Oscar thinks to touch the kid, to put a hand on his head, but before he does, Javi wraps his arms around his shoulders. He opens his mouth and speaks.

"Couldn't keep his big mouth shut," Javi says, and it's not sweat coming from his eyes. "Had to fucking say something. Had to get out of the car. What the fuck was he gonna do, Oscar?"

Something's burning inside Oscar then, something like pride and love and joy, the thought of Marcel hustling across an icy sidewalk and howling some shit to strung-out Tomás. The sight of his brother's mouth open wide, those big-ass teeth, stark white and hope-to-God catching the sun, and that tongue of his just letting fly whatever song he came up with to drive out the night, to push against that bastard. Tomás probably didn't know he'd pulled the trigger. Probably didn't even hear the fire pop and the bullet jump over the sound of Marcel's absurd caw.

Oscar moves to Javi then and grabs the boy's shoulder with his left hand. He presses his rough, stubby fingers into the boy's skin and does his best to steady him. There's some juice in the boy. Oscar can feel it in the muscle over the bone. He's sure he can feel the two-day's rest in how fast the welterweight twitches.

"Oye," Oscar says now without whispering.

Javi's knuckles have turned white on his shoulders, doing their best to hold on despite the tape and the sweat. He does not seem to have heard Oscar.

"How are your legs?" Oscar asks. "How are your legs, Javi? Did you run yesterday or Wednesday?"

It takes a minute but the boy eventually shakes his head no.

"Good. Did you drink a beer yesterday? Did you walk home?"

Javi nods, and Oscar can feel him settling onto the bench, but his arms stay in place, his hands still stuck on his shoulders.

"Did you sleep in this morning?"

The taped hands relax and Oscar can see blood return to the knuckles, flood the fingers.

"Yeah," Javi manages.

"Bien," Oscar says. "Two months and now it's time, okay?"

"Okay," Javi whispers.

"But listen, you know all that shit I said about finding a stance? Picking a spot and punching from it?"

Javi nods.

"Don't worry about that tonight."

The boy looks up at Oscar with wide eyes, and Oscar feels okay taking his hand off of Javi's shoulder. He needs to stiffen his own back now. And Oscar is busy taking the scorecard from his front pocket and scribbling the boy's name on it. He doesn't look at Javi as he does this, but keeps talking.

"Just try to get comfortable in there, and if that means moving your ass all over the ring, then fine. You got your feet tonight. You got your legs. Let them run if it feels all right."

Javi lets his arms drop, and his chin follows. His breathing slows, and Oscar watches the boy's frame rise and fall while sliding the card back into his pocket.

"Then what?" Javi asks.

Oscar doesn't hesitate.

"Then you throw some punches when he gets tired. If you see his nose, swing. If not, cover up. Keep your face clean. Just make sure to cover up. Don't let him get at your face." Oscar takes a breath. "Stay pretty, all right?"

He puts a hand on the boy's head.

Javi nods.

*　　*　　*

Javi follows Oscar through the hallway that leads out into the arena. The passage is as cramped as the locker room, and pipes run the length of the ceiling. Water runs through them and, at a few rusty joints, it leaks out onto the floor in small, patient drops. The concrete is slick, and the shine washing in from the open door to the center stage turns the look of the puddles into ice.

Javi follows Oscar's lead and walks on his toes, stepping around the wet spots. He needs to keep his boots dry. He needs to be ready to move, to run, to do what Oscar's told him to. It's from one brother to the next, and Javi feels like a toy passed between siblings. Oscar's hand on his head and the love something like the same. Javi considers for the first time that Oscar has shown up at his fight; the brother faithful as if his corner presence was a test of his loyalty to Marcel. In all likelihood it is just that, which is another way of saying that he won't be there forever. One fight in memoriam, maybe a handful more for propriety; he will not ask for more. With Marcel gone, he no longer has a good reason for getting his face smashed in. He thinks to make the fight perhaps a good one.

Oscar walks more slowly than his brother did, takes shorter, heavier steps, and Javi remembers how quick he had to tiptoe to keep up with Marcel. He'd follow him out of bed, share that cup of five-thirty coffee, and do the rounds with el jéfe. Ride shotgun in Marcel's clean Cutlass and move from one silver coffee cart to the next. They'd pull up to a curb and park almost on top of a fire hydrant, no traffic or police cramming the streets just yet. Catch a vendor putting the stand together, getting the cups ready and polishing the red, white and blue flag on the cart's side. Marcel would leap out of the car and pounce on the man with his booming voice and wide open mouth, and Javi would follow. Marcel's clear open eyes dead set on his vendor, never bloodshot, never tired, juiced already. Slow-shifting but white as his teeth and never drooping, not even on the coldest days of December.

"Javi, this is Freddy. His stand is brand new last Monday. Brand fucking new! See how that thing shines? Like the moon on fire! How you like it so far, hombre?"

The vendor smiled like a puppy that still pisses everywhere and said, "It's okay."

"Just okay?! You got to make it better than 'okay,' Freddy! This shit is your livelihood. It is my livelihood! You been calling out to people? You been squawking at the sun when they walk by?"

"Sometimes," Freddy said.

"Fuck sometimes!" Marcel screamed. "We're gonna do it right now. We're gonna wake this street up! Take a breath, Freddy. You got to scream if you want to keep your cart. You fucking ready?"

"What do I do?"

"You know 'oye'? Means listen up in Cuban. That's what you scream because you got something to say. Listen, fuckers! I got coffee here! I got the coffee! People don't know what they're missing if you don't tell them, Freddy!"

Javi laughed behind Marcel, and he could see Freddy's face turn a little red.

"All right, hombre, you ready? The loudest fucking 'oye' of your life."

Javi looked up and down the street to see who would hear Freddy's best attempt at Marcel, but there was no one. A couple of cars coming their way, and it was cold out, all the windows in the surrounding buildings locked tight. Who would hear the boy make a noise? Even a gunshot would sink into the pavement.

"Oi-yay!" Freddy tried, and it was sad and flinty and had nothing on Marcel. But the big teeth were out, and Javi saw how firm and loving Marcel could be. He saw without a doubt the size of Marcel's chest and how much room he made for others, and he felt lightheaded thinking the tuft of hair just north of the sternum his own private place.

"Not bad, hombre! Every day, Freddy, I want to hear your voice when I'm getting out of my car. You see me pull up to the curb, you better warm up that tongue of yours. I want it flapping, even in the cold, even if the tip starts to freeze. You got me?"

"Yes, Marcel," and the boy nodded furiously, happy to have his job, happy to have made a sound, happy to have said something in front of el jéfe.

Marcel kept it up, kept talking on the way to the car, getting louder the further from the stand they got so the vendor wouldn't miss a word.

"Up with the sun, Freddy, and that's a lot of competition! Got to be louder than light!"

With no crowd out in the bleachers, Javi thinks the lamps will be the loudest noise in the arena tonight. White noise to keep everything down and subdued until the sharp ping of the starting bell. The lamps will wash out the stage and then bleach his opponent's face, drain the blood out of the red-colored ropes. The mat will be warm to the touch. Not a bad place to lie down. Not a bad place to fall if he gets tagged.

Oscar looks over his shoulder as they near the light. "Okay?"

Javi nods.

Oscar's told him to run, but Javi can't imagine running under these lights. They're too hot, and his opponent isn't a sparring partner. He isn't going to stop when Oscar puts his hands up or spits enough.

Javi follows his trainer up blue stairs and under a stretched rope. He spies the other man still in his robe and throwing ghost jabs in the opposite corner. Javi sees his gloves, checks his shoes, and watches his calves for bounce and speed. The fighter follows his own four-part shadow, and his knees, trailing his punches, poke out from under the robe. The man's trunks are green and bright against his cocoa skin. Javi doesn't remember the last time he looked so hard. He'd become accustomed to being seen rather than seeing, but he knows this isn't urge as much as it is necessity.

Still, the man is beautiful. Javi hadn't gotten much of him in the sparsely lit locker room, and under these lights his opponent is clearly in better shape than he is. A little more padding on the chest, a little more width in the forearms, a few more dimples striating the abdomen. Dangerous, Javi thinks, and perhaps Oscar is right.

The man is also hairy. Black curls gather in a tuft at the sternum but then descend in a tapering column towards his stomach. They stop there, dipping into his navel and absorbing what sweat works its way down from the man's obliques. Javi forgets a moment that the arms on either side are meant to hit him and instead imagines the scent that escapes the green trunks when that torso shifts against the waistband. Breaths of wet air. Javi imagines getting close.

The referee comes by to check his gloves, and Javi has to look away. He's getting instructions, ones that will be repeated before the first bell. The man examines the laces at his cuffs, pushes a thumb into the meaty part of the red leather, pats Javi on the shoulder and walks away.

Javi knows what it would take to get close. Oscar's trained him to claim the space between two men. When he started, Javi just walked right up to sparring partners and started swinging, no pause in his gait or interlude for thought, and if he landed one, he'd run. Oscar's shown him since to stop once he's two or three feet from the other guy's face, to rear up and study his opponent then, see which direction his feet tend to move and notice which arm floats an inch lower than the other. Get close, but stop yourself, and Javi hates the approach. It lets the pressure build, allows the oxygen to get heavy, makes taking that space a terrifying act of will.

The two fighters, mouths masked by bobbing leather gloves, blow anxious breath out their lungs and through their noses. The panting mixes with the sweat on their arms, the moisture on their chests, and sags between them like a summer storm. A hard place to get to, the fighter working between jabs and body shots, but worth it if he can get inside the other's reach. Because then he can move and throw like a lucky fool. Close enough not to worry about heavy hooks or full wind-ups. No need to chase, the man right there. Oscar's told him to run, but now Javi thinks otherwise. He can feel their knees bumping up against each other. He's starting to smell the sweat off the other man, and he will pick a spot and punch, peck his way into the space between.

Acknowledgements

Thank you to Erin McGraw, mentor and friend, for her always wise and illuminating counsel. Thank you to my peers at the Ohio State University, especially Gabe Urza, sparring partner extraordinaire, for your careful, considerate and supportive comments on the early drafts of this piece. Thanks to Deena Drewis for her incomparable editor's eye which made possible and palpable all the good things in this work.

Immense gratitude to my family, both near and far, to whom this book is dedicated. Your presence brought me to Cuba, which in turn brought my writing there. Special thanks to my parents, Debra and Carlos, and to my siblings, Dan and Aubrey, for their continued love and support. Lastly, thank you, Claire Vaye.

Derek Palacio was born in Evanston, IL, in 1982 but grew up in Greenland, NH. He holds an MFA in Creative Writing from the Ohio State University. His work has appeared in *Puerto del Sol* and *The Kenyon Review*, and his story "Sugarcane," was selected for inclusion in The O. Henry Prize Stories 2013. He is the co-director, with Claire Vaye Watkins, of the Mojave School, a non-profit creative writing workshop for teenagers in rural Nevada. Currently, he lives and teaches in Lewisburg, PA, where he is completing a novel about a small Cuban family struggling to remain whole after fleeing the island as part of the 1980 Mariel Boatlift. He is also working on a collection of short stories relating to Cuba's past, present and future.